My Pretty Ballerina ®

Saturday Is Ballet Day

By Karen Backstein • Illustrated by Cathy Beylon

SCHOLASTIC INC.

New York   Toronto   London   Auckland   Sydney

To Nancy and "Spike"

ISBN 0-590-45143-X

Copyright © 1991 by Tyco Industries, Inc.

My Pretty Ballerina trademark and likeness used under license from Tyco Industries, Inc.

All rights reserved. Published by Scholastic Inc.

12 11 10 9 8 7 6 5 4 3 2 1   1 2 3 4 5 6/9

Printed in the U.S.A.   2 4
First Scholastic printing, September 1991

Saturday is my favorite day of the week.
That's because Saturday is ballet day.
And I love ballet.

Even the clothes are wonderful!
At the ballet school, I quickly put on my
leotard, and tie the ribbons of my pink satin
toe shoes.

I just can't wait to dance!
That's why I'm always the first one here.

All alone in the room, I jump and spin and
stand on the tips of my toes.
When I shut my eyes, I can even imagine the
audience watching me.

In my dreams the crowd applauds and
applauds.
"More! More!" they shout.
It sounds so real!

"Very good!" someone calls out.
It is my ballet teacher, Miss Marie.
Beside her stands a new girl. She looks scared.

"Good morning, Miss Marie," I say as I curtsy.
You always curtsy when you greet your ballet
teacher.

"Hello, My Pretty Ballerina," Miss Marie
smiles. "I'd like you to meet someone.
This is Jordan. Today is her first ballet class."

Jordan smiles shyly. "I don't know anything about ballet."
"Would you like me to show you some steps?" I ask.

"Oh, yes!" cries Jordan. "Then I'll know what to
do when class begins."
I lead her to a wooden bar attached to the wall.
"All ballet words are in French," I explain,
"and this is called the *barre*.
We always begin our exercises here."

"First, put your hand on the barre. That will help
you keep your balance.
Then, place your heels together just like this.
That's first position."

Jordan tries to copy my steps.
She wobbles a little at first.
But she's catching on.

"Here's second position."

"And this is third."

"Now slide your foot forward—and you're in fourth!"

"Fifth position is the last one.
It's very hard."

Whoops!
Jordan is all tangled up!

"I can help you straighten out.
Try it this way."

Jordan is learning to love ballet as much
as I do!
"Can I learn some more steps?" she begs.
I show her a *plié*.
"Just bend your knees. Be sure to stand very
straight!"

Nothing is more beautiful than an *arabesque*.

We twirl and twirl in *pirouettes*.

Finally, we leap across the room in *grand jetés*.
It's just like flying!

Now Jordan is all smiles.
"Ballet is great!" she grins.
"And so are you!"

I can hear the tinkling sounds of the piano.
I know what that means!
"Class is about to start. Let's go join the others
so you can get a good place at the barre."

Now there are lots of dancers in the room.
Some are practicing difficult steps.
Others are beginners.
Suddenly Jordan looks frightened again.

"Don't worry," I say calmly.
"I'll come and dance with you."

Jordan and I dance the whole class together.
And when we do our jumps, no one flies higher
than Jordan!
Not even me.
Saturday is still the best day of the week.
Saturday is ballet day—and the day I see my
new friend.

First Position

Second Position

Third Position

Fourth Position

Fifth Position

Plie (Plée-AY)

Arabesque (Ah-re-BESK)

Pirouette (Peer-ooh-WEHT)

Grand Jeté (grahnd zhe-TA'